HALFWAY WILD

WRITTEN BY
LAURA FREUDIG

ILLUSTRATED BY
KEVIN M. BARRY

ISLANDPORT PRESS

Text © 2016 by Laura Freudig
Illustrations © 2016 by Kevin M. Barry

Published by Islandport Press
P.O. Box 10
Yarmouth, Maine 04096
books@islandportpress.com
www.islandportpress.com

ISBN: 978-1-934031-48-3
Library of Congress Control Number: 2016931238
Printed in Canada by Friesens Book Division
Production Date: July 2016
Job # 224749

To Ben, Emma, Daniel, Kate, and James,
who are wild and wonderful
—LAURA FREUDIG

For my family
—KEVIN M. BARRY

We have lived on the
same bumpy road
in the same white house
since before I was born,
but we are never
the same from
one day to
the next.

When the morning sun shines in through
the slats of our window shades
and we start to buzz and tumble,

we're a family of
BUMBLEBEES.

When the sweetest cereal
is on the highest shelf,

we're a family of
MOOSE.

When our socks sag
and our pants are wrinkled,

we're a family of
TURTLES.

When there is more paint on us
than on our pictures,

we're a family of
PUFFINS.

When we spring from one side of the living room to the other without touching the floor,

we're a family of
SQUIRRELS.

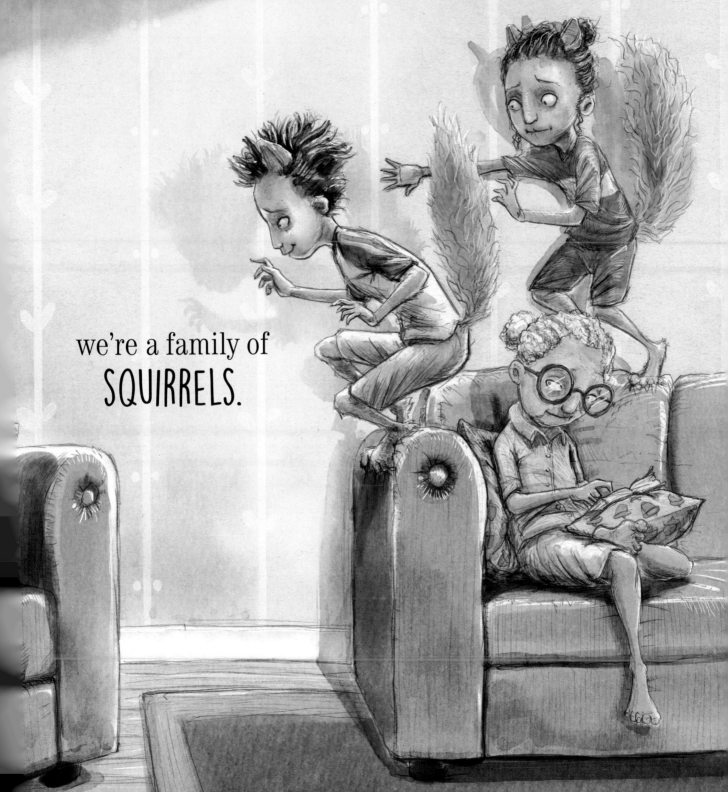

When puddles call, we're a family of
DUCKS.

When we march in a ragged line
through the meadow
to the sea,

we're a family of
ANTS.

When our lunch disappears
with two swallows and a squawk,

we're a family of
SEAGULLS.

When we dive from sunlight
to cool green depths,

we're a family of
SEALS.

When we scurry home through
the tall grass,

we're a family of
FIELD MICE.

When we eat spicy food
and have to drink water to cool
the fire on our tongues,

we're a family of
FOXES.

When we play hide-and-seek until
the stars come out,

we're a family of
FIREFLIES.

When no one can remember the last time
we took baths,

we're a family of
SKUNKS.

When we can't stop chattering even after
we are buttoned and brushed and tucked into bed,

we're a family of
RACCOONS.

And when the house is still
and all we can hear are the soft, slow breaths
of the ones we love,

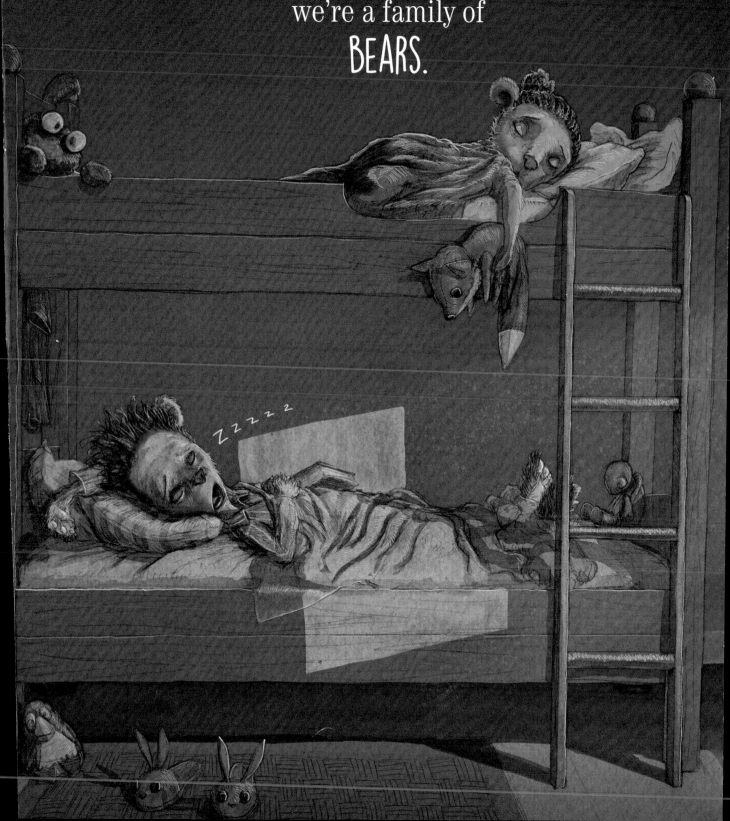

Night deepens in our white house.
We shed feathers and fur, and return
from sea and sky.

We settle into our skin and dream—of the
creatures we have been and those
we will be tomorrow.

ABOUT THE AUTHOR

Laura Freudig lives on an island along the Maine coast with her husband, six children, two ducks, fifteen chickens, one dog, and one very wild cat. She likes reading, singing, hiking, and gardening.

Photo by Kevin Bennett/Islandport Press

ABOUT THE ARTIST

At an early age, Kevin M. Barry began drawing crazy cats and martial artist monkeys on the backs (and corners) of his homework assignments, a habit he has yet to break. When not illustrating books, the award-winning children's book artist can be found either scratching out stories with elementary students; snout deep in a book; or exploring the wilds of New England with his own *Halfway Wild* family.

Photo by Elizabeth Barry